D0394697

Tumbleweed Stew

Tumbleweed Stew

Susan Stevens Crummel

Illustrated by Janet Stevens

Green Light Readers
Harcourt, Inc.

Orlando   Austin   New York   San Diego   London

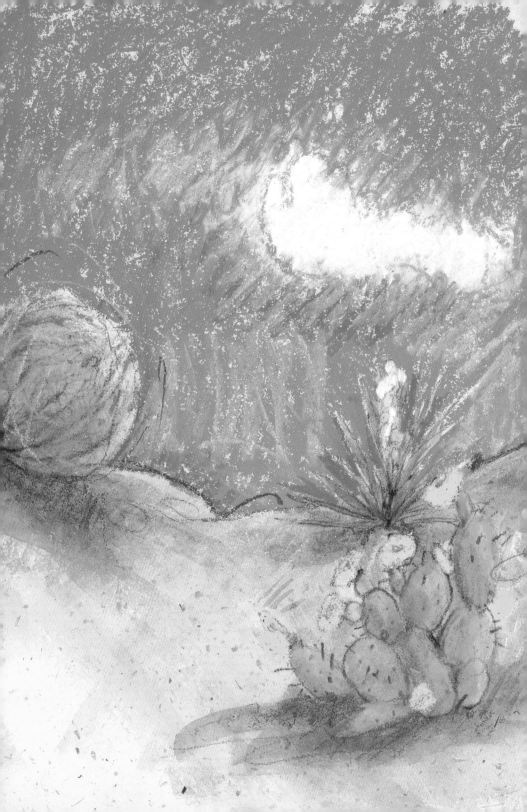

Jack Rabbit opened his eyes. He stretched and looked up at the pretty blue sky.

Jack's tummy growled. He thought,
The sun is up. The sky is blue!
What a great day for tumbleweed stew!
He hopped along, jumping over brush
and cactus.

Before long, he came to a big gate. Over the gate it said TWO CIRCLE RANCH. Jack slipped under the fence and into a herd of cattle.

"Moo!" said Longhorn. "Move on!"
"Well, howdy," Jack said. "How do you do?
How would you like some tumbleweed stew?"

"There's no such thing as tumbleweed
stew," said Longhorn, munching the
dry grass.

Not a nice place, thought Jack. He ran
down the path to the ranch house.
"Anyone home?" he called.
"*No!*" he heard from inside. "Go away!"
"How about some lunch?" asked Jack.

Armadillo came out onto the porch. "This is my ranch," she said. "This is my food and you can't have any!"

Jack took a chance. He said,
  "But I would like to cook for *you*.
    Have you heard of tumbleweed stew?"
"There's no such thing as tumbleweed stew,"
Armadillo said.

Before Armadillo could blink, Jack started a fire. He spied an old pot and filled it with water. He set the pot of water on the fire. After a while, he stuffed a big tumbleweed into the pot.

Armadillo looked into the pot. Jack took
a taste and said,
"It smells so good. It tastes good, too.
But it needs more, this tumbleweed stew."
"Well," said Armadillo. "There might be some
carrots in my house."

Soon the tumbleweed

and carrots

were cooking
in the big pot.

Buzzard floated down to take a look. "I can smell this food way up in the sky! It needs onions," he said. "I'll fly home and get some."

Soon the tumbleweed,

carrots,

and onions

were cooking
in the big pot.

Then Deer trotted over and looked into the pot. "This stew needs corn," he said. "I'll be right back."

Soon the tumbleweed,

carrots,

onions,

and corn

were cooking
in the big pot.

Skunk scampered up to the pot. "Smells good," she said. "But where are the potatoes? I'll go dig some up."

Soon the tumbleweed,

carrots,

onions,

corn,

and potatoes

were cooking
in the big pot.

Rattlesnake slithered over with some celery. "You can't make stew without celery," he said.

Soon the tumbleweed,

carrots,

corn,

onions,

and celery

potatoes,

were cooking
in the big pot.

Armadillo, Buzzard, Deer, Skunk, and Rattlesnake gathered around the pot of stew. They watched it bubble and steam.

At last Jack cried,
    "It took a while, but thanks to you,
    It's time to eat this tumbleweed stew!"
The animals ate and ate until every bite of
stew was gone.

Armadillo couldn't move. Buzzard couldn't fly.
Deer couldn't trot. Skunk couldn't scamper.
Rattlesnake couldn't slither.
They put their heads down and fell asleep.
Jack slept, too, but not for long.

Jack Rabbit opened his eyes. He stretched
and looked up at the pretty blue sky.
His tummy growled. He thought,
Another day for being sly—
What a great day for cactus pie!

Think About It

 1 How does Jack Rabbit get the other animals to put vegetables in the stew?

2 Would you want to have Jack Rabbit for a friend? Why or why not?

3 What did you learn about the characters from looking at the pictures? What else do the pictures tell you?

Make a Tumble-Snack

WHAT YOU'LL NEED

pretzels	raisins	popcorn	nuts

small plastic bags   measuring cup   large self-closing plastic bags

Tumble-Snack

3 cups popcorn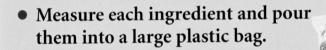

1 cup nuts

2 cups pretzels

2 cups raisins

- Measure each ingredient and pour them into a large plastic bag.

- Close the bag. Shake the bag to "tumble" your snack.

- Pour or scoop out the snack into small bags.

Now eat your delicious

Tumble-Snack!

Meet the Author and Illustrator

Ted Habermann

Susan Stevens Crummel

Janet Stevens

Susan Stevens Crummel and her sister, Janet Stevens, grew up all over the United States, including Texas, where *Tumbleweed Stew* takes place. The sisters worked together on the story. Susan wanted the characters in the story to be animals that live in Texas. Janet kept drawing them until she liked the way they looked. "The best part of making this story was working with my sister," says Janet.

Requests for permission to make copies of any part of the work should be
submitted online at www.harcourt.com/contact or mailed to the following address:
Permissions Department, Houghton Mifflin Harcourt Publishing Company,
6277 Sea Harbor Drive, Orlando, Florida 32887-6777.

www.HarcourtBooks.com

First Green Light Readers edition 2000
Green Light Readers is a trademark of Harcourt, Inc., registered in the
United States of America and/or other jurisdictions.

The Library of Congress has cataloged an earlier edition as follows:
Crummel, Susan Stevens.
Tumbleweed stew/Susan Stevens Crummel; illustrated by Janet Stevens.
p. cm.
"Green Light Readers."
Summary: Jack Rabbit tricks the other animals into helping
him make a pot of tumbleweed stew.
[1. Rabbits—Fiction. 2. Tricks—Fiction.] I. Stevens, Janet, ill. II. Title.
PZ7.C88845Tu 2000
[E]—dc21 99-50803
ISBN 978-0-15-204870-9
ISBN 978-0-15-204830-3 (pb)

C E G H F D B
E G I K L J H F (pb)

Ages 5-7
Grades: 1-2
Guided Reading Level: G-1
Reading Recovery Level: 17

Green Light Readers

For the reader who's ready to GO!

"A must-have for any family with a beginning reader."—*Boston Sunday Herald*

"You can't go wrong with adding several copies of these terrific books to your beginning-to-read collection."—*School Library Journal*

"A winner for the beginner."—*Booklist*

Five Tips to Help Your Child Become a Great Reader

1. Get involved. Reading aloud to and with your child is just as important as encouraging your child to read independently.

2. Be curious. Ask questions about what your child is reading.

3. Make reading fun. Allow your child to pick books on subjects that interest her or him.

4. Words are everywhere—not just in books. Practice reading signs, packages, and cereal boxes with your child.

5. Set a good example. Make sure your child sees YOU reading.

Why Green Light Readers Is the Best Series for Your New Reader

● Created exclusively for beginning readers by some of the biggest and brightest names in children's books

● Reinforces the reading skills your child is learning in school

● Encourages children to read—and finish—books by themselves

● Offers extra enrichment through fun, age-appropriate activities unique to each story

● Incorporates characteristics of the Reading Recovery program used by educators

● Developed with Harcourt School Publishers and credentialed educational consultants

Look for more Green Light Readers wherever books are sold!